A Mouse in the House

T0337185

Written by Jillian Powell

Illustrated by Valeria Abatzoglu

Collins

What's in this story?

Listen and say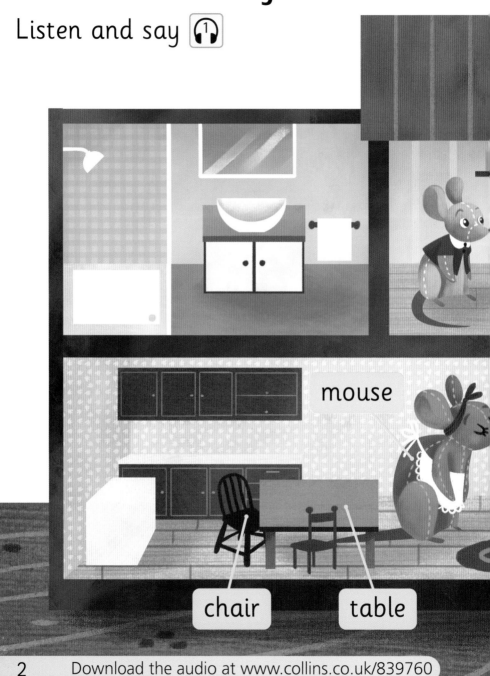

mouse

chair

table

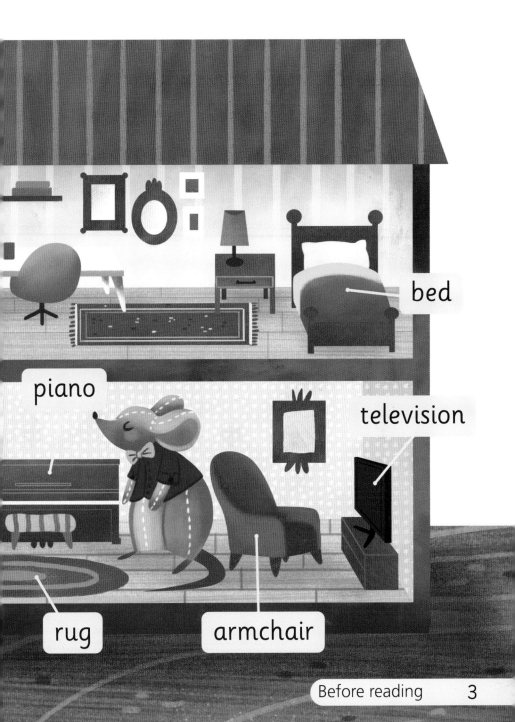

bed

piano

television

rug

armchair

Mum is sleeping in the armchair.
Yoyo the cat is sleeping there.

Look! Clare sees a small mouse.
It's running under Mummy's chair.

Where is that small grey mouse, Clare?
Is it under the armchair?

No, no, it's not there.

Is it behind the television?
Clare can't see.

No, the mouse is not there.
Where can it be?

Is the mouse under the table?
Does it want some tea?

Shh, Clare! Yoyo is sleeping! And we don't want Mum to see!

Is the mouse under the piano?
Is it between the piano legs?

Is it under the hats and coats?
Quick, Clare, look on the pegs!

Is it under the bed? No, it's not there.

There is a mouse in the house.
But where?

It is not in the bedroom.
It is not behind the door.

It is not under the rug on Clare's bedroom floor.

What do mice like? Where can it be?

Clare goes to the kitchen.
What can she see?

Clare goes into the garden. Goodbye, small grey mouse! Go!

A mouse in the house? *Ssh!* Mum and Yoyo don't know!

Picture dictionary

Listen and repeat

armchair

bed

in

mouse

rug

table

television

under

1 Look and order the story

2 Listen and say

Collins

Published by Collins
An imprint of HarperCollins*Publishers*
Westerhill Road
Bishopbriggs
Glasgow
G64 2QT

HarperCollins*Publishers*
1st Floor, Watermarque Building
Ringsend Road
Dublin 4
Ireland

William Collins' dream of knowledge for all began with the publication of his first book in 1819.

A self-educated mill worker, he not only enriched millions of lives, but also founded a flourishing publishing house. Today, staying true to this spirit, Collins books are packed with inspiration, innovation and practical expertise. They place you at the centre of a world of possibility and give you exactly what you need to explore it.

© HarperCollins*Publishers* Limited 2020

10 9 8 7 6 5 4 3 2

ISBN 978-0-00-839760-9

Collins® and COBUILD® are registered trademarks of HarperCollins*Publishers* Limited

www.collins.co.uk/elt

British Library Cataloguing in Publication Data

A catalogue record for this publication is available from the British Library.

Author: Jillian Powell
Illustrator: Valeria Abatzoglu (Beehive)
Series editor: Rebecca Adlard
Publishing manager: Lisa Todd
Product managers: Jennifer Hall and Caroline Green
In-house editor: Alma Puts Keren
Project manager: Emily Hooton
Editor: Deborah Friedland
Proofreaders: Natalie Murray and Michael Lamb
Cover designer: Kevin Robbins
Typesetter: 2Hoots Publishing Services Ltd
Audio produced by id audio, London
Reading guide author: Sarah Jane Lewis-Mantzaris
Production controller: Rachel Weaver
Printed and bound by: GPS Group, Slovenia

MIX
Paper from
responsible sources

FSC
www.fsc.org

FSC™ C007454

This book is produced from independently certified FSC™ paper to ensure responsible forest management.

For more information visit: **www.harpercollins.co.uk/green**

Download the audio for this book and a reading guide for parents and teachers at www.collins.co.uk/839760